How to H
a
Meadow Frog

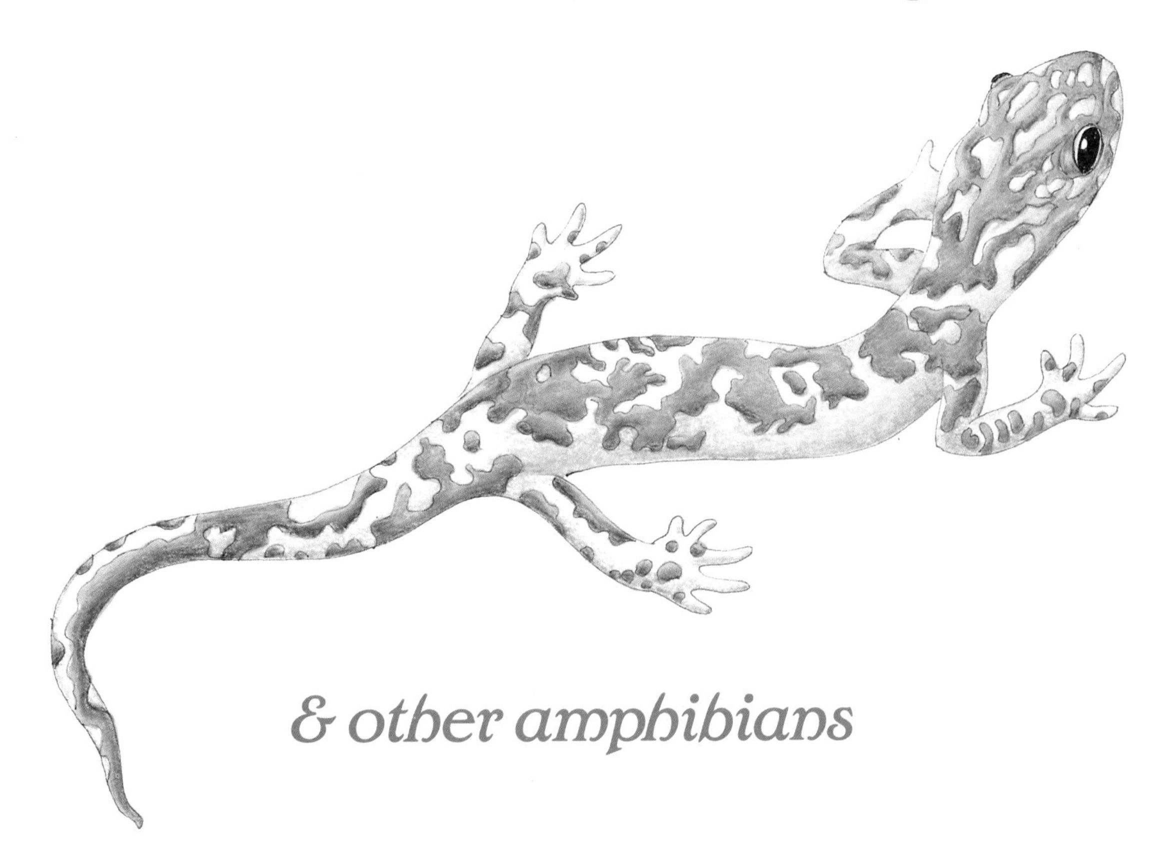

& other amphibians

A Grosset & Dunlap **ALL ABOARD BOOK**®

With special thanks to
Robert C. Drewes, Ph.D.
Chairman
Department of Herpetology
California Academy of Sciences

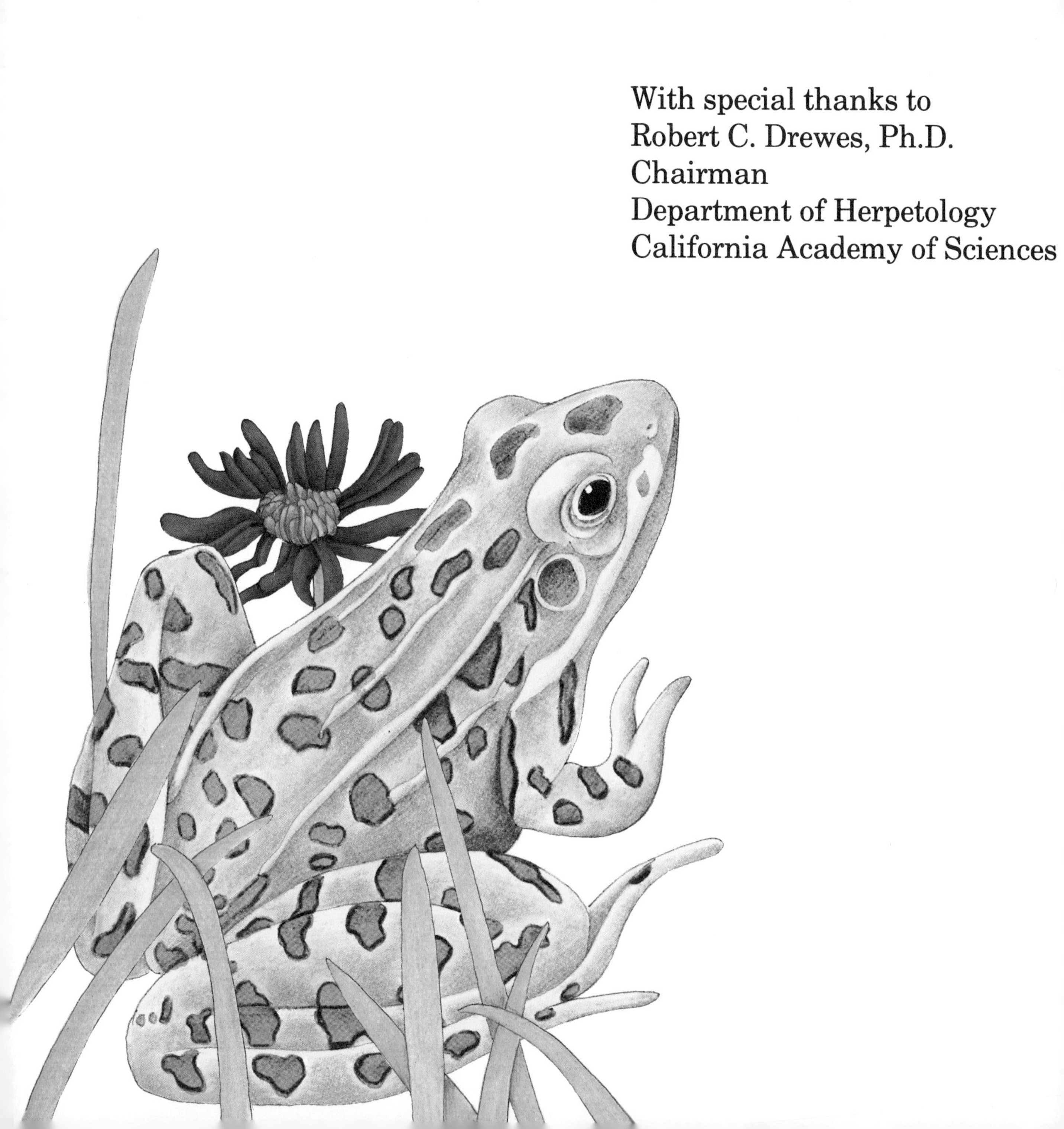

If
you take
a careful look,
you'll see
how
creatures
in this book
are
CAMOUFLAGED
and out
of view—
although
they're
right
in
front
of
you.

RUTH HELLER'S

How to Hide a Meadow Frog & other amphibians

Originally published as How to Hide a Gray Treefrog & Other Amphibians

Grosset & Dunlap, Publishers

 Originally published in smaller hardcover edition as HOW TO HIDE A GRAY TREEFROG & OTHER AMPHIBIANS. Published by Grosset & Dunlap, Inc., a member of The Putnam & Grosset Group, New York. GROSSET & DUNLAP is a trademark of Grosset & Dunlap, Inc. ALL ABOARD BOOKS is a trademark of Grosset & Dunlap, Inc. Registered in U.S. Patent and Trademark Office. THE LITTLE ENGINE THAT COULD and engine design are trademarks of Platt & Munk, Publishers, a division of Grosset & Dunlap, Inc. Published simultaneously in Canada. Printed in the U.S.A. Library of Congress Catalog Card Number: 94-78865 ISBN 0-448-40965-8
A B C D E F G H I J

The
GRAY
TREEFROG
is
quite
a
clown.
It leaps about,
then
settles
down.

With suction cups
upon its toes,
it clings to things.
Then off it goes.

Depending
on the
temperature,
the
dampness,
or
the
light…

it's sometimes gray
or
green or brown
and sometimes pearly white.

The
MEADOW
FROG
is...

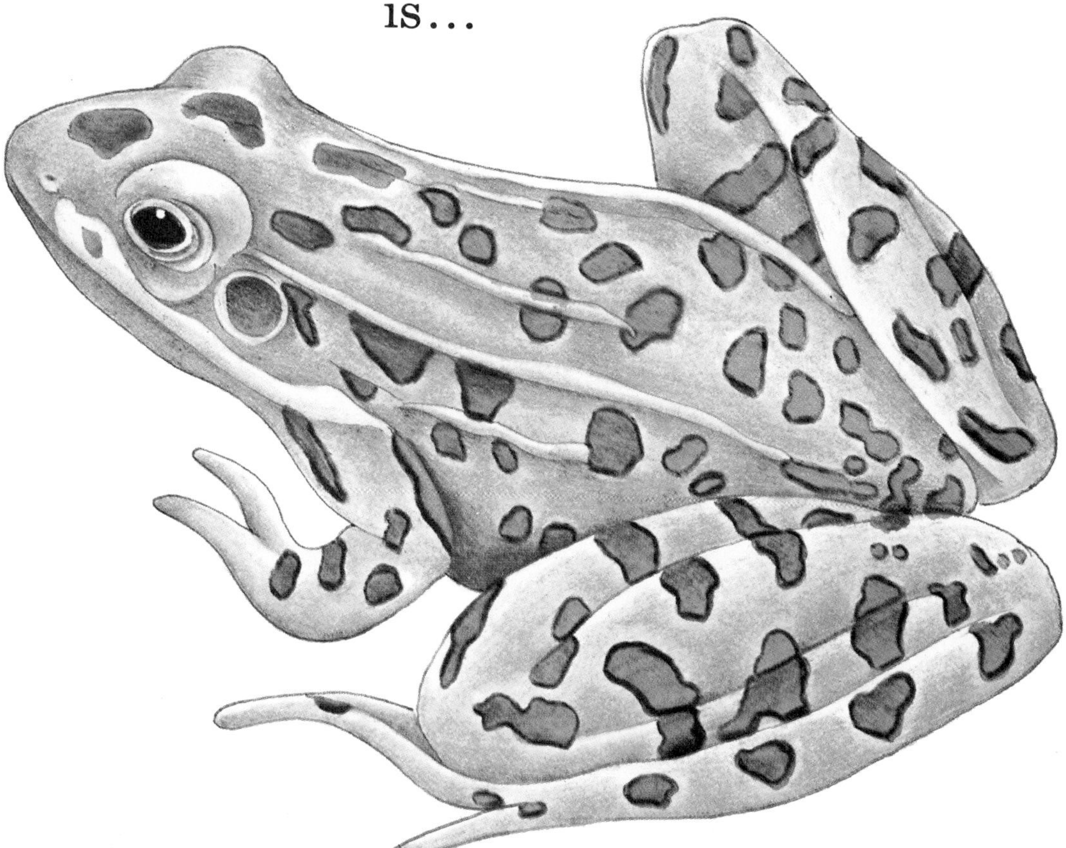

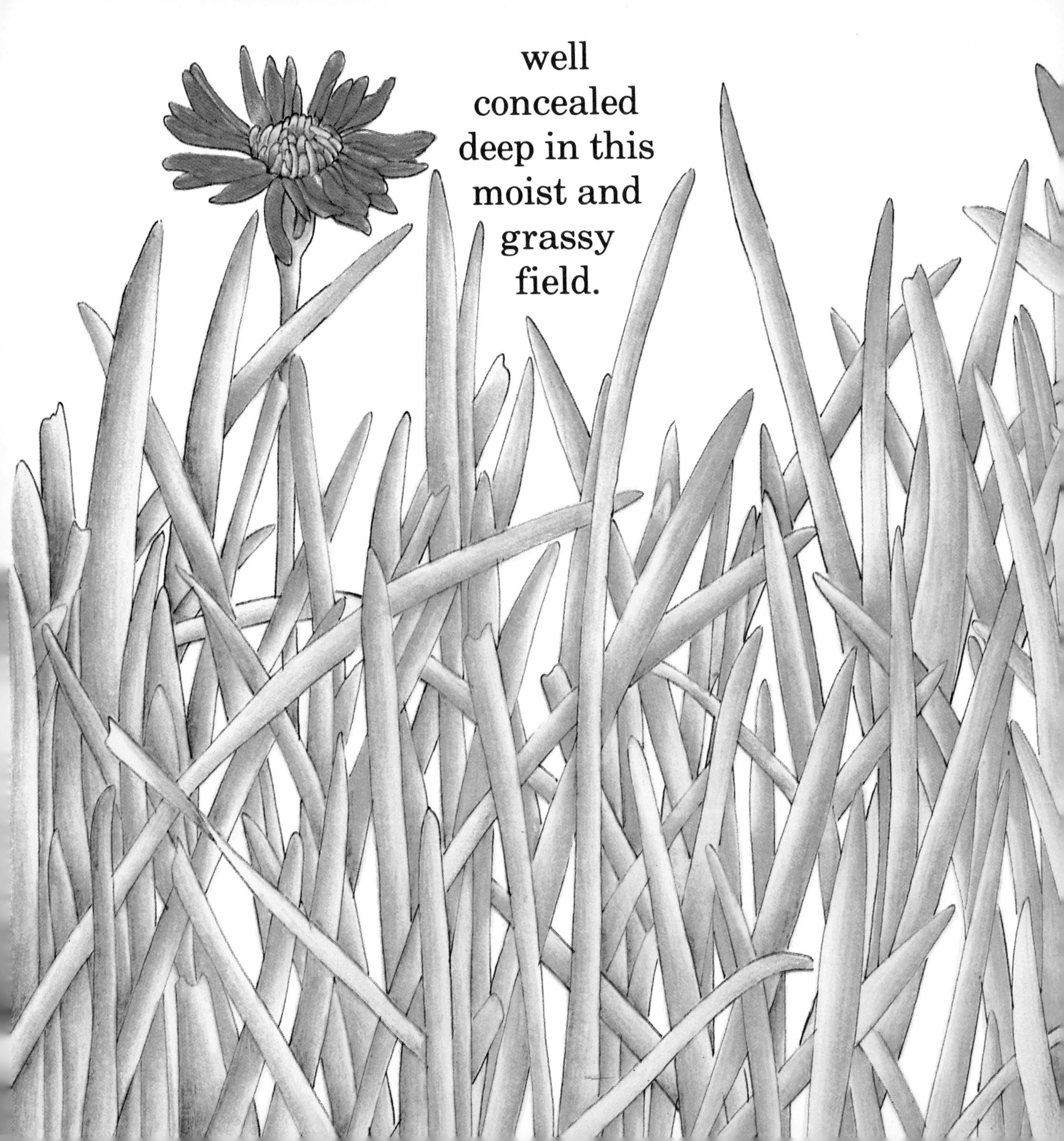
well
concealed
deep in this
moist and
grassy
field.

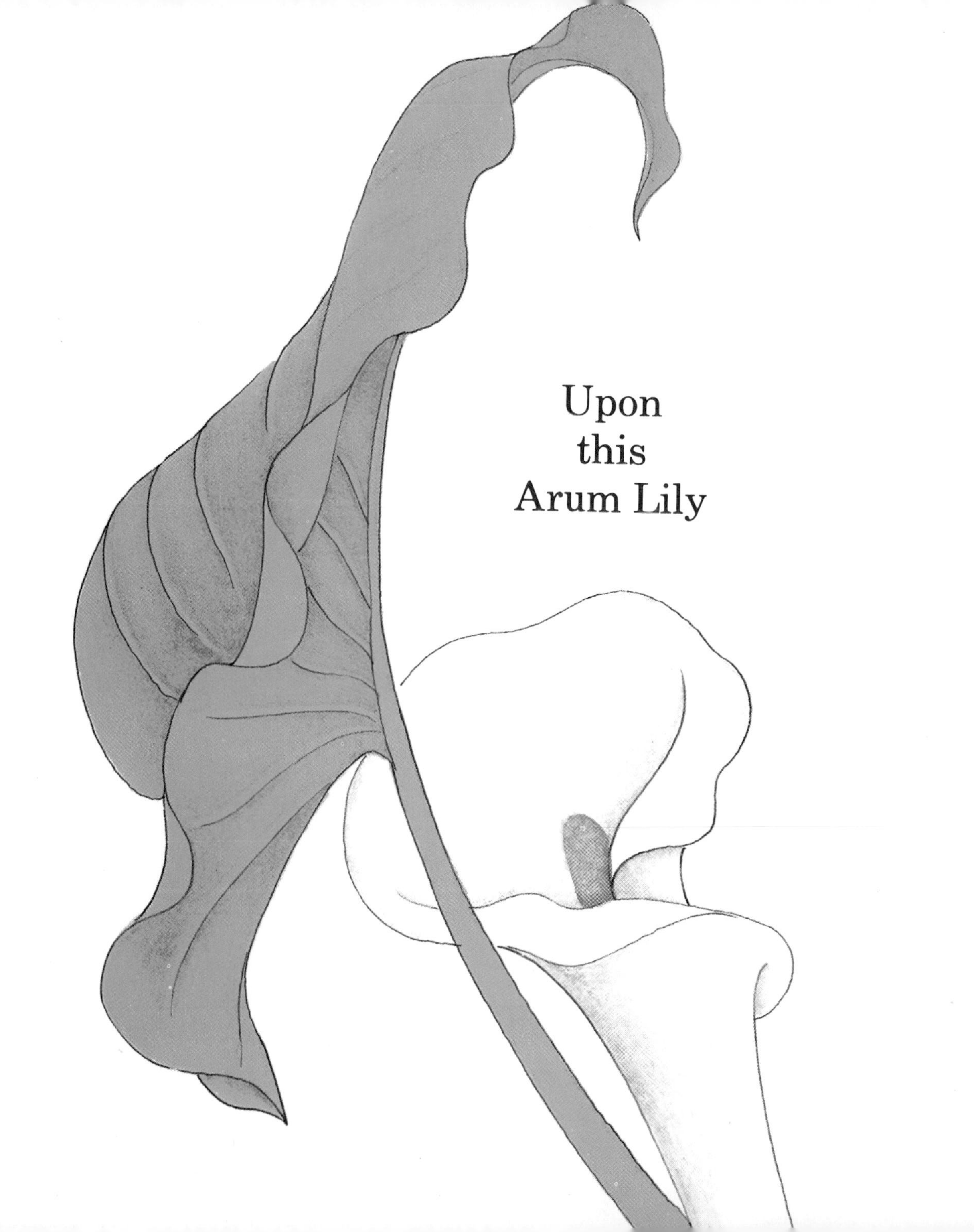

Upon
this
Arum Lily

will
this
ARUM
FROG
alight…

where it will stay
and
nestle
down

and
turn
from
brown
to
white.

It is quite
beyond belief.

The
HORN
FROG
looks…

just like a leaf.

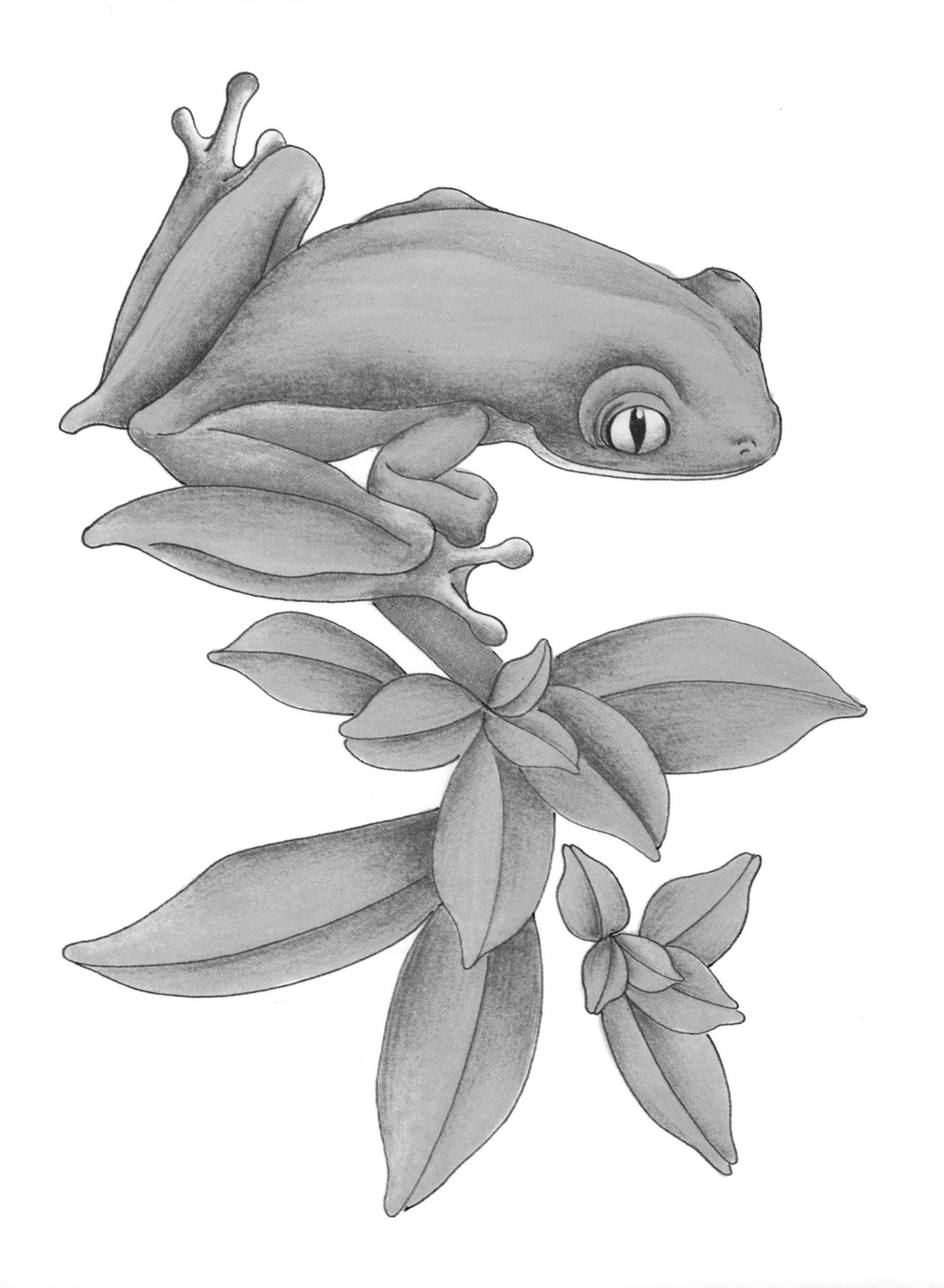

This
is
a
CAT-EYED
TREEFROG
from
the
jungles
of
BRAZIL.

His
legs
are
shaped...

to
hide
him
when
he
is
sitting
still.

All
the
splendor
that's
bestowed
upon
this
well-designed
GREEN
TOAD
can

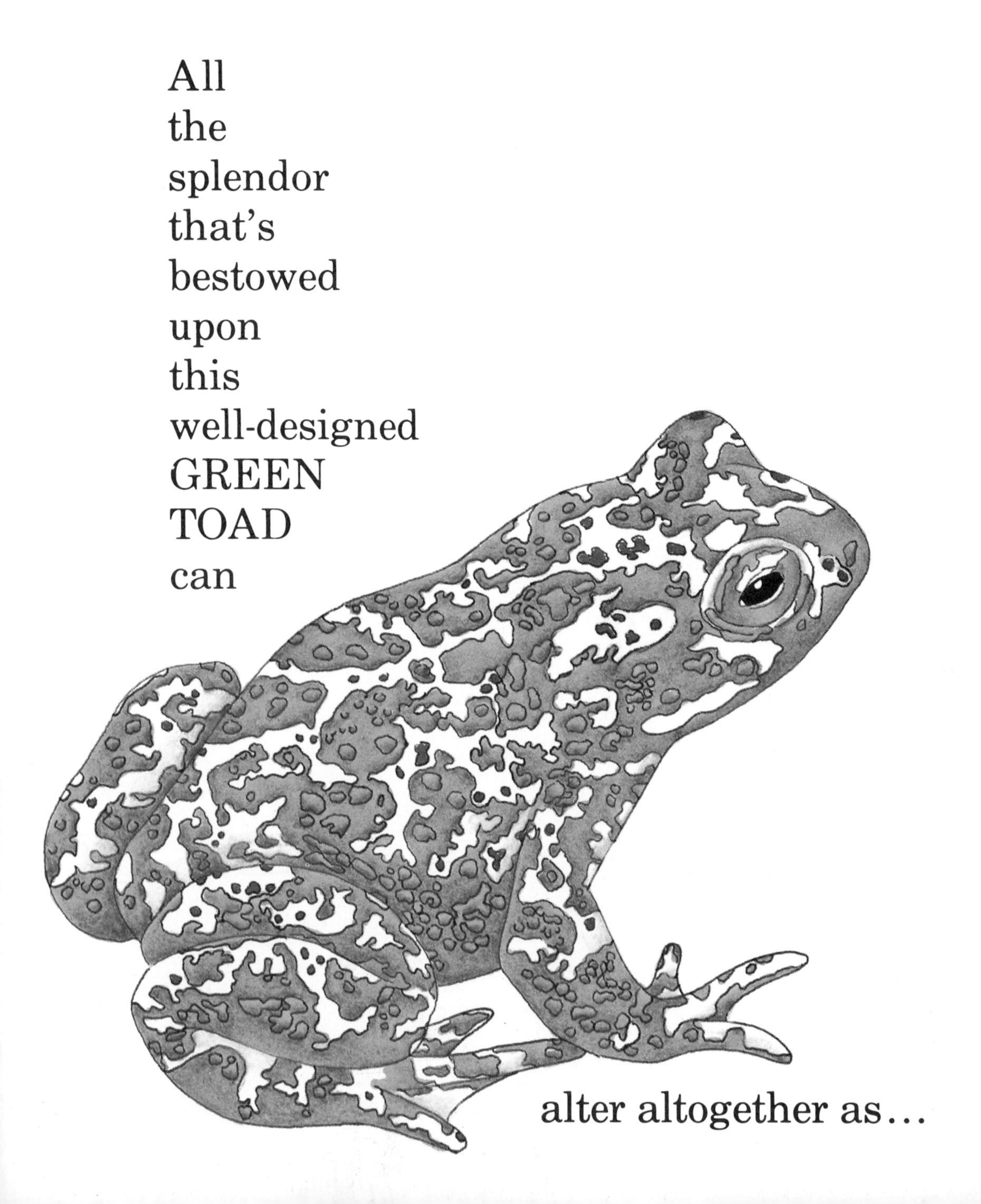

alter altogether as...

you see it fade away
to become a pasty gray.

Looking
like
the
lichen
where
it
likes
to
live,
this
SALAMANDER

can
be
sure…

that it is really quite obscure.

Because the world is
hostile,
all creatures need
protection.
They need to hide
so thoroughly
that they defy detection.

So…
some of them use
camouflage
to fade away with ease
from predators
who like to dine
upon these predatees.

But…
predators
to live must eat,
so
also fade and are
discreet,
and then their prey
on which they sup
can't see
who's going
to eat them up.